BEESMASHER

B.I. PHILLIPS

To order additional copies of this book, contact:
Xlibris
844-714-8691
www.Xlibris.com
Orders@Xlibris.com

ISBN: Softcover   978-1-6698-4290-3
       EBook   978-1-6698-4289-7

Print information available on the last page

Rev. date: 08/22/2022

Grateful acknowledgements to
West Village Dog Park.

This book belongs to:

_____

One day while taking a break between sets a cute honey bee landed on my tennis racquet which was leaning against the bench.

5

I thought to myself that sweet bee is reminding us to play more tennis.

All of a sudden a tennis racquet came out of no where and smashed him.

I was so upset. I left and reported what had happened.

The nice girl I was playing with came to console me and said she was allergic to bees.

Later I sent her an article that they were harmless. She thought I should call the book the bee smasher.

After this I went out to the West Village Park to utilize my anger management skills. What had this affected! Was it my financial security and/or my emotional security and/or both. It was not my financial security, but my emotional security. I prayed that this resentment would be removed.

While there I noticed turtles sitting on branches. What message were they trying to convey?

A few weeks later after playing another match I notice a yellow jacket hovering around the base line. What was he/she trying to tell me? Lines like an actress or actor would read? Or something else?

Upon returning home I noticed a spider had built an intricate web adjoining the dome light in the garage. It was three dimensional. Likely waiting for the bugs to flock to the light which disturbed me. Or possible trying to tell us to build our own houses and get our own food. After a few weeks I couldn't deal with it anymore and Peter relocated the spider. Then I was sad because the spider had become my friend.

The following morning a rabbit in the grass stopped to look at me.

19

This morning while feeding the birds i watched the birds go after the apple danish. I couldn't BELIEVE when I saw the bird take the too tough apple danish piece down to the water and wet it to make it softer. Incredible thinking process!!!

A O R A N G E R M O A Q
S B C B W E B S X R F P
M T E C C D F K D A F O
A R L E A O I I R N D N
A M T D I V A L I G C M
S P R A B E E L B E A K
H O U C X Z L S I L L Z
E C T T N E M E G A N A M
R X C E A F O E Y E B C D
E N P N B C T D A N I S H
M L S N X Z H I Z O S K P
F X L I M P S X M Q E Q L
A X M S A L L F N R B S V
Z

Printed in the United States
by Baker & Taylor Publisher Services